SS

D1077236

This book
belongs to

....

Muddle
The Magic Puppy

THE MAGIC CARPET

Muddle
The Magic Puppy

THE MAGIC CARPET
by Hayley Daze

Willow
Tree

A CIP catalogue record for this book is
available from the British Library

This edition published by Willow Tree Books, 2018
Willow Tree Books, Tide Mill Way, Woodbridge, Suffolk, IP12 1AP
First published by Ladybird Books Ltd.

0 2 4 6 8 9 7 5 3 1

Series created by Working Partners Limited,
London, WC1X 9HH
Text © 2018 Working Partners
Cover illustration © 2018 Willow Tree Books
Interior illustrations © 2018 Willow Tree Books

Special thanks to Jane Clarke

Willow Tree Books and associated logos are trademarks and/or
registered trademarks of Tide Mill Media Ltd

ISBN: 978-1-78700-440-5
Printed and bound in Great Britain
by Bell and Bain Ltd, Glasgow

www.willowtreebooks.net

For Daniel and Charlotte,
my two curious adventurers

When clouds fill the sky and rain starts to fall,
Ruby and Harry are not sad at all.
They know that when puddles appear on the ground,
A magical puppy will soon be around!

Muddle's his name, he's the one
Who can lead you to worlds of adventure and fun!
He may be quite naughty, but he's clever too,
So come follow Muddle – he's waiting for you!

Contents

Chapter One
The Naughty Puppy

Ruby hopscotched down Grandad's garden path, splashing her way through the puddles. Her wellies sent the water spraying high into the air. Ruby loved how the dots of mud splattered on her dress and the raindrops caught in her braids. *Yes*, thought Ruby.

*If there was an Olympic puddle jumping
competition, she would definitely be
the world champion!*

Ruby zigzagged along the final
stretch of path, racing towards an
imaginary finish line, but just as
she reached the last puddle, a puppy
splashed right into the middle of it,
soaking her.

"Hello!" Ruby said, smiling and
wringing out her braids. "Where did
you come from?" She leaned down to
check the puppy's neck for a collar, but
he didn't have one. "Are you lost?"

The puppy shook his head.
Raindrops flew from his floppy ears.

Muddle
The Magic Puppy

"Would you like to play with my cousin Harry and me?" Ruby asked. The puppy raced Ruby up the garden path. They burst through the front door of Grandad's cottage and into the living room.

Harry was sitting in the window seat, reading a puzzle book. He looked up and pushed back his glasses, which had slipped down his nose. "I don't think puppies are allowed in the house," he said, looking worried. "Especially not wet puppies with muddy paws!"

The puppy bounced around the room, knocking over Harry's pile of library books and Grandad's umbrella stand. He ran up to Harry and snatched the puzzle book right out of his hands.

"Hey, you give that back," Harry called, but he was grinning. "You're not just muddy, are you? You're naughty too!"

Harry chased the puppy and Ruby chased Harry. Ruby and the puppy left a trail of muddy prints across Grandad's living room floor, which was now littered with books and umbrellas.

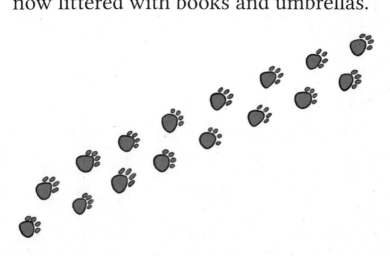

The puppy came to a sudden stop in the middle of the Persian rug. Harry fell over the puppy, tumbling head over heels, and Ruby fell over Harry. They all lay on the rug in a tangle of arms, legs – and a happily wagging tail. The puppy wriggled free, dropped the book in front of Harry, and licked him on the cheek. His bright eyes sparkled with mischief.

"Yuck," Harry cried, picking up his puzzle book by the corner. "It's all slobbery."

"Come on, Harry," Ruby begged. "The puppy just wants to play, and so do I. We've been stuck in Grandad's cottage for two whole rainy days. And

the rain still hasn't stopped!"

There were dark clouds in the sky and Ruby pointed at the raindrops running down the window panes.

But Harry stood up, dusted himself off, and returned to the window seat. He opened his puzzle book and started reading. Harry loved reading more than anything.

Ruby sighed – then smiled when she saw that the puppy was nipping playfully at the tassels on the corner of the rug. Every time he pulled

at a tassel, he rolled over on to his back. Ruby knelt down and rubbed his tummy.

"You want to roll up in the rug, don't you?" she said. "So do I!"

Ruby lay down on the rug and rolled over and over so the rug became a tube with just her braids hanging out.

"Help! Harry!" Ruby cried in a muffled voice. "The Giant Carpet Monster has got me."

The puppy jumped on top of the rolled-up rug. Ruby could feel his wagging tail bumping against it.

Ruby squealed and wiggled her wellies inside the rug. She squirmed along so she could poke her head out of

the end. Her messy braids swung back
and forth as she tossed her head and
shouted, "Save me!"

"That is not a Giant Carpet
Monster," Harry said. "That is
Grandad's old Persian rug."

Ruby immediately stopped wiggling. "It's make-believe," she said.

"I don't believe in make-believe," Harry said.

"How could you not ..." Ruby started to say, but the puppy began to tug on the frayed edge of the rug with all his

might. Ruby rolled free and landed
with a thump against Grandad's coffee
table, toppling the dish of peppermints
and scattering the contents of Harry's
pencil case on the floor.

"I told you he was a naughty
puppy," Harry said, hopping down and

gathering his collection of pencils and
coloured pens.

"My hero," Ruby said, hugging
the puppy a little too tightly. "You
saved me!"

The puppy wriggled free and dashed
back outside, with Ruby close behind.
The rain was falling heavily now. One
of the raindrops landed with a plop on
the tip of Ruby's nose. Others slid down
her cheek, her dress and even into the
toes of her wellies.

"Come on, Harry," Ruby called. She
watched him pull on his wellies and
peer into the garden.

"It's too muddy to play outside,"
Harry said, looking down at his nice

white shirt and his pressed beige trousers.

The puppy ran towards Harry, splashing through the puddles, and jumped up to his chest. Harry nearly fell over.

"Urgh!" groaned Harry, wiping mud from his shirt. "I don't think I've ever been this filthy in my life." But he was smiling happily, and he bent to stroke the puppy's soggy ears.

"I think he likes you," Ruby said. "I wonder what his name is."

"We should call him Muddle," Harry said. "He's certainly turned Grandad's

cottage into a muddle!"

"Would you like that name, boy?" asked Ruby.

The puppy offered her a muddy paw.

"That's a deal, then. Muddle it is," Ruby said, shaking his paw. She and the puppy splashed in every puddle on the path, Ruby's braids bouncing up and down. "Come on, Harry, try this. It's great fun!"

Harry wiped specks of muddy water from his glasses. "I don't think so," he said.

Muddle barked and danced circles round a big puddle. Ruby skipped over, splashing water into the air as

she went.

The puppy looked from Ruby to Harry.

"Stop him," Harry groaned. "He's going to jump."

But the puppy leapt into the puddle and ...

Ruby gasped and looked at Harry. His eyes were wide as he stared at the puddle.

"Muddle's disappeared!" they said together.

Muddle
The Magic Puppy

Chapter Two
Muddle Makes a Splash

The puddle was still rippling around the spot where Muddle had jumped in. "Where did he go?" Ruby asked, dropping to her hands and knees. All she saw was her reflection, made topsy-turvy in the muddy water. "He's vanished."

"He can't have done," said Harry, scratching his head.

"Well, I'm going in after him." Ruby stood up tall, straightened her dress and tugged on her braids for luck.

"I don't think that's a good idea – " Harry began to say.

But Ruby swung her arms back. "Here I go ..."

"Wait for me!" said Harry.

Ruby grabbed her cousin's hand, and with a shimmering splash they jumped, wellies first, into the puddle.

***

Ruby and Harry landed with a thud on a shabby carpet. For a moment, Ruby thought she was back in Grandad's cottage, playing on his old Persian rug. But then she heard Muddle bark. He wagged his tail and looked happy to see her. Ruby stroked his head.

"Where are we?" Ruby asked.

Muddle barked and jumped over Ruby and Harry, landing right in the lap of a young boy. He was sitting cross-legged at the far end of the carpet, staring wide-eyed at them through the fringe of his dark hair. Harry adjusted his glasses and waved nervously.

"Where did you come from?" the boy asked.

"We're really sorry to drop in on you like this," Ruby said. "I'm Ruby, and this is Harry and that –" she pointed to Muddle – "is Muddle, the naughtiest puppy I've ever met."

The boy laughed and tickled Muddle's chin. "I'm Aziz," he said.

Ruby and Harry could not believe the sights and smells as they looked around. The sun bounced off white-walled buildings and painted roofs. Ruby could smell delicious spices and orange blossom. "We're definitely not in Grandad's village any more," she said.

Suddenly the carpet began to ripple. The ground seemed to shift below their feet. Muddle raced from one side of the carpet to the other, while Ruby, Harry and Aziz bounced up and down as if the carpet had become a trampoline. Harry lost his balance and tumbled on

to his front. He rolled to the edge of the carpet and looked over.

"Ruby," Harry said with a gulp, "we're not on the ground."

"We're flying!" Ruby gasped, and squealed with delight. She scooped up Muddle, who licked her face. He seemed to like flying as much as Ruby did.

Aziz laughed at their excitement. "This is my flying carpet," he said. "Hold on tight!"

They zoomed over a bustling market-place filled with flowers, fruit, pottery and brightly coloured rugs. In the distance Ruby could see a palace with a shimmering golden dome.

Muddle

The Magic Puppy

"It's beautiful," Ruby said. "Look at all the tall towers with the onion-shaped tops!"

"Minarets," Harry said. "They're called minarets. I read it in a book." Ruby tilted her head and looked at her brainy cousin. "Minaret. Sounds like the name for a sweet." She licked her lips. "A kind of twirly watermelon-and-grape-flavoured lollipop."

She heard a whizzing sound behind them.

"Watch out!" shouted a loud voice. They felt a bump as something knocked into their carpet and sent it spinning off in another direction.

"What was that?" Ruby cried.

Muddle barked at something nearby. Ruby turned and saw a swarm of flying carpets gathering over the market-

place. Carpets of every size and colour circled above the excited crowd.

"Flying carpets – hundreds of them!" Ruby shouted. She grabbed Muddle and hugged him close to her chest. "Isn't this wonderful?"

Chapter Three
The Magical Race

Harry wiped his glasses again and again, as if he couldn't believe his eyes. "It's amazing," he said, "but it's also impossible. Carpets can't fly. There must be engines on them somewhere." He pushed his glasses back into place and tried to peek under the carpets.

"Or it could be magic!" Ruby said.

"This isn't a real flying carpet, is it?" Harry asked.

"Oh yes, it's real," Aziz said, "and it goes really fast. Hold on!"

Suddenly, Harry was thrown across the carpet. All the flying carpets were zooming forward. Ruby grabbed on to Harry and Muddle grabbed hold of a bit of carpet with his teeth.

"It's a magic carpet race!" Ruby shouted. They sped through the air, making Ruby's braids take flight. Muddle's ears flapped in the wind.

"I don't mind flying, but maybe not quite as fast as this," said Harry, now lying flat on the carpet like a starfish.

Ruby thought he was starting to turn a little green.

Aziz's flying carpet shot past other racers above and below them. The crowd in the market-place cheered.

Aziz leant forward and the carpet plunged downwards, like a rollercoaster speeding down a hill. Ruby and Harry gripped the tassels of their carpet tightly. Ruby's stomach jumped and danced. She liked the feeling. It made her want to scream and giggle all at once.

But Muddle wasn't holding on. The little puppy rolled past Ruby, tumbling over and over.

"Oh no," Ruby cried. "Muddle can't stop!"

She scrambled towards him but she was too late. Muddle had toppled over the side!

Aziz levelled the carpet and Ruby

heard a muffled yelp.

"Muddle? Is that you?" She looked over the edge.

Muddle was dangling underneath, clinging to a single thread of the carpet.

Chapter Four
Ruby to the Rescue

"Hang on, Muddle!" Ruby shouted.
She hooked one arm under the puppy's
body and held tightly to the carpet
with the other. Harry grabbed Ruby's
legs to steady her. But Aziz had to
make another sharp turn to avoid a tall
rooftop. Ruby lost her grip and Muddle

flew high into the air.

"Muddle!" Ruby screamed as she dived to the back of the carpet and reached over the side. Muddle landed in her outstretched arms.

"I've got you," she whispered to the puppy as she lifted him safely back on to the carpet.

"Is he OK?" Aziz asked, pushing his hair back off his face. Muddle barked and wagged his tail. They all laughed.

"This is some race," Harry said to Aziz. "What do you get if you win?" Ruby saw that Harry now looked slightly less green.

"The winner will be granted one wish by Princess Amber," Aziz said.

"Are you going to wish for a new flying carpet?" Ruby asked, poking her finger through one of the carpet's many holes.

Aziz darted past another racer.

"My family's carpet is very old, but still very fast," he said proudly.

"I can see that!" Harry said. "So what would you wish for?"

"I must keep it a secret for now," Aziz said, rounding another corner, "or it might not come true."

Muddle barked loudly as a thick red carpet, ridden by a girl in a turquoise dress, hurtled by and overtook them.

"Oh no you don't," Aziz said. "Hang on, everyone. Here we go again!"

By now they were all good at holding on tight as Aziz picked up speed. He was soon gaining on the other carpet.

"Aziz, watch out for those minarets

ahead," said Harry, his voice
shaky again.

Aziz grinned. "That's exactly where
we're going!"

Muddle hid his face beneath his
paws.

Chapter Five
A Close Finish

Aziz swung his carpet round so it was racing straight towards the towers.

"My carpet's smaller than that girl's thick red carpet," he shouted. "I can go between the minarets, but she'll have to go around them."

Ruby stroked Muddle's ears, and

the puppy uncovered first one eye and then the other. Aziz's eyes narrowed as the minarets grew closer and closer. Muddle barked and nipped at the edge of the carpet. He pulled it in towards Ruby, Harry and Aziz.

"Muddle's right," Aziz called. "Quick, pull in the sides; it's going to be a tight squeeze."

Ruby and Muddle grabbed one side and Harry quickly tugged on the other. Their carpet raced smoothly right between the minarets!

"Wow, you're an amazing carpet flyer, Aziz!" Ruby said. She looked at the other flying carpets they would have to pass to win the race. Aziz was

Muddle

The Magic Puppy

definitely the youngest racer.

"I can't find a gap that I can get through!" Aziz called to Ruby and Harry. "We'll have to slow down."

As Ruby and Harry searched the skyline for a carpet-sized space, Muddle barked loudly. He pointed his whole body, nose first, towards a patch of blue sky.

"Well done, Muddle," shouted Ruby.

"It's going to be tricky," Aziz said, pushing the hair from his eyes. "I'm not sure I can steer the carpet through such a small gap!"

"We can help," Harry said. "If we put all our weight on one side, it'll make the carpet turn better. I read about it in

my physics book."

"Just like surfing," Ruby said, scrambling to her feet and balancing on the carpet. "Let's do it!"

"Well, actually, surfing uses water, not air," Harry corrected her. "But it's the same thing, I suppose. Now, everybody lean right!"

Ruby, Muddle and Harry all leaned to the right. Muddle was clinging to Harry, and Harry was clinging to Ruby. The carpet started to tip, and Aziz sped past two of the other racers.

"Now left!" Harry yelled.

They rolled to the opposite side, Muddle grabbing the hem of Ruby's dress with his teeth. Aziz zoomed

past three more racers, and the carpet slid through the gap that Muddle had pointed out. The tassels of Aziz's carpet brushed the other carpets as they passed.

"That was close," Ruby said. "I can see the finish line, there on the roof of the palace!"

"It's not over yet," Aziz said. "There's still one more racer ahead of me, and he's really fast."

Aziz sped up and soon the two carpets were racing neck and neck, neither one able to take the lead. They were only a few carpet lengths from the finish.

"We must be able to go faster," said Ruby. "But how?"

Muddle hopped from Ruby's lap and rolled along the carpet. Ruby reached for the puppy, but Muddle barked and backed away, out of her reach. He shook his head from side to side and then rolled over again. He grabbed the edge of the carpet in his teeth and began to roll himself inside it.

"Muddle," Harry groaned. "You'll fall off again."

But Ruby realised what the puppy was doing. "That's it!" she shouted. "If the carpet was shaped like a rocket, long and thin ..."

"That's a great idea," Aziz shouted. "You're a genius, Muddle!"

He steered the carpet left and then quickly rolled it right, spinning them round and round. The carpet rolled into a tube with the friends tucked safely inside.

"Woooaaaah!" shouted Ruby and Harry together as the carpet raced forward, rocketing towards the finish line.

Chapter Six
The Princess's Problem

The rolled-up carpet zoomed over the finish line just ahead of the other racer. Ruby, Harry, Muddle and Aziz all spilled out on to the palace roof, laughing as the magic carpet unrolled itself.

"You did it!" Ruby cheered.

"We all did it," Aziz said. "A special thanks to you, Muddle!"

The sound of a gong filled the air and a willowy young girl stepped out of the golden dome on the palace roof. She walked slowly towards them, her long yellow dress and orange silk veil blowing in the wind.

"That's Princess Amber," Aziz whispered to his new friends. He stepped forward and bowed.

Ruby and Harry copied Aziz. Muddle lowered his head too.

"Please rise," Princess Amber said. "I must congratulate you on winning the flying carpet race."

"*Shokran*, Princess – much thanks,"

Aziz said. "I am Aziz and these are my ..." He paused. "My friends, Ruby and Harry." Muddle barked. "Oh, and who could forget Muddle?"

"*Salaam*, Princess," said Harry. Princess Amber nodded.

"What did you say?" Ruby whispered to Harry.

"It's 'hello' in Arabic," Harry said. "I took a few Arabic lessons last year before I started French."

Muddle
The Magic Puppy

Muddle bowed and the princess
reached down to stroke him.

"You all raced with courage,"
Princess Amber said, "and you truly
deserve the prize." She looked away.
The princess's eyes were cloudy
and sad.

"Excuse me, Your Highness, but is
something wrong?" Ruby asked.

Princess Amber sighed. "It's my
magic lamp," she said.

"So many things are magic around
here!" Ruby said. "Lamps, carpets ... do
you have magic shoes as well?"

Ruby was pleased to see Princess
Amber give a small smile. Then the
princess held up a golden lamp. "It is
an old oil lamp that I was given for my
birthday," she said. "Inside it is a magic

genie who grants wishes." Her smile faded. "But he won't come out."

"Wow, there's a genie in there?" Ruby stared at the lamp.

"And the genie will grant Aziz his wish?" Harry asked.

"Yes," the princess replied, "if you are able to remove him from the lamp." She gently placed it on the ground in front of them.

Muddle barked at it crossly.

"Muddle," Ruby said, "the genie won't come out if you're rude to him."

Muddle licked the lamp and rubbed against it.

"Whooo, hoo, haaa, haaa," a voice echoed from deep within the lamp,

which began to shake from side to side.
"No, stop please! Haaa, haaa! It tickles!"

Muddle shot behind Harry's legs and peeked out at the quivering lamp.

"Maybe there's some secret button that opens it?" Harry said, pressing a square marking on the top. Then he wiggled the handle, turned the whole lamp upside down, and pressed the circles underneath and the diamond

shapes on the sides.

"Uuurp!" burbled the lamp as a wisp of greenish smoke came out of the spout. "Please stop. You're making me lamp-sick."

"Sorry," Harry said. He gently turned the lamp right-side up again.

"It's hopeless," sighed the princess.

"Wait!" said Ruby, taking the lamp from Harry. "It's a magic lamp, right? Maybe there's a magic word."

"I've already tried," Princess Amber said. "I tried all the magic words I know – Abracadabra, Alakazam and even Open Sesame. But none of them worked."

Now it was Aziz who hung his

head and looked sad. "I understand, Princess," he said. "I will not get my wish."

Chapter Seven
Granting Aziz's Wish

"There must be something we can do," Ruby said, pacing back and forth across the palace roof.

Muddle was scampering about on the patterned tiles, chasing his tail and barking. He knocked into a refreshment table, sending oranges and cakes rolling

across the floor.

"Muddle, you naughty puppy," said Harry. "Keep still and let us think, please!"

With a low rumbling sound, the lamp began to shudder. They all turned towards it.

"That's it!" Ruby exclaimed, picking up the lamp and raising it over her head. "The most magical word of all is ... *please*."

White smoke poured from the lamp's spout.

The smoke twirled into the shape of a large, round genie. The genie floated above the lamp, still connected to it by a swirl of smoke from the spout.

"You did it," said Princess Amber, her eyes shining with happiness. "Thank you!"

Ruby stared at the genie. "Wow, you're much bigger than I thought you'd be," she said.

"Are you saying I'm fat?" asked the genie. "Look, there's not much room to exercise in that lamp."

"Sorry," said Ruby nervously. "You look great. Very magical and swirly."

"You think so?" the genie said. "You don't think all the smoke is too much?"

Muddle barked and shook his head.

"Dear Genie," Princess Amber said, "now that you are here, will you please grant our wish?"

"Why do people always jump straight to the wishing?" the genie asked, shaking his head. "Not even a how-do-you-do or a cup of tea. A genie can get mighty thirsty in that tiny lamp."

Ruby could see Princess Amber pull her orange veil round to cover a smile. "My apologies, Genie," the princess said. "But Aziz has won the magic carpet race and your first wish belongs to him."

"Winning a race isn't so special," the genie said with a frown. "I could fly pretty fast when I was young." He zoomed left then right, up then down, leaving a trail of smoke behind him.

"What a grumpy genie," Ruby whispered to Harry.

"I heard that," the genie said, landing next to Ruby. "I don't feel like granting any wishes today."

Muddle began to growl. He even nipped at the trail of smoke the genie left behind.

"Muddle's right," Ruby said, wagging her finger at the genie. "You aren't being very nice."

"I think granting wishes must be fun," Harry said. "You get to make people happy."

"Yes," Ruby agreed. "What an amazing power to have!"

The genie puffed out his chest and

beamed at them. "I guess you're right," he said. "I do like granting wishes!"

Muddle trotted across the roof to a marble staircase and barked.

Princess Amber turned to the friends. "Everyone is waiting to meet you," she said, picking up the lamp, with the genie floating above it. "Will you join me for the wish-granting ceremony?"

They descended the marble staircase, which led down from the palace roof on to a stage decked in

brightly coloured banners. The cheers
of a huge crowd filled the air.

Princess Amber stepped forward.
"May I present the winner of the magic
carpet race – Aziz!"

Aziz's magic carpet floated onto
the stage with a sparkling silver trophy
resting on top. The princess took the
trophy and handed it to Aziz.

"Aziz, please tell me – what is your
wish?" Princess Amber asked.

Aziz brushed his hair from his face.
"I wish for a new house that is big
enough for my whole family to live in
together," he said.

The genie was bowing and waving
at the crowd. When Ruby gave him

a nudge, he clapped his smoky hands together and Aziz's family magically appeared on the stage – his mother, father, brothers, sisters, aunts, uncles, cousins and even his cat.

"I suppose you want your own room, too?" the genie whispered to Aziz.

Aziz smiled and nodded.

"Your wish is granted," the genie boomed, pointing into the distance. An arrow of smoke whizzed to the hillside and exploded, creating a huge heart-shaped cloud.

The smoke cleared to reveal an enormous white house with blue doors and lilac flowers trailing up the walls.

Muddle
The Magic Puppy

It was perfect!

"That's for us?" Aziz gasped.

The genie laughed. "It certainly is."

The applause of the crowd filled the air. The sound was louder than any thunderstorm Ruby had ever heard.

"I'm so happy that you got your wish," Ruby shouted over the noise. Muddle gave a happy bark as if he agreed.

"I couldn't have done it without all of you," Aziz shouted back.

Harry tugged on Ruby's sleeve. "There's just one problem."

"What could possibly be wrong?" Ruby asked. "We've won a magic carpet ride, met a princess and a genie,

and Aziz and his family have a new home. What more could anyone wish for?"

"Aziz has his new home," Harry said, twisting his hands together. "But we don't know how to get back to Grandad's cottage!"

Ruby realised that Harry was right. How would they ever get home?

Chapter Eight
Muddle's Magic

Muddle barked and began to race in circles round and round Ruby and Harry.

"What is that crazy puppy doing?" Harry asked.

Ruby looked at Muddle and felt her stomach go all fizzy, like the bubbles in lemonade. "Look!" she said. "The world's gone all fuzzy."

"It's like looking through a rain shower," Harry said.

Aziz and his family, Princess Amber and the genie became a blur as the puppy ran even faster.

Ruby grabbed Harry's hand. "I think Muddle is taking us home," she cried.

Ruby and Harry both called "Goodbye!" to their new friends, and could just hear them shout farewell in return. Ruby's skin tingled and her braids began to spin. Then she closed her eyes against the whirlwind Muddle was creating.

***

When Ruby opened her eyes again, she saw the most beautiful sight in the world, even more beautiful than the minarets – it was Grandad's cottage. She and Harry were standing among the puddles on Grandad's garden path.

"That was ... unbelievable," Harry said, smoothing his hair and straightening his glasses.

"But where's Muddle?" Ruby asked, looking around for the naughty puppy.

"He's disappeared again," Harry said. He peered into the puddles. "Maybe he wasn't real. Maybe none of it was."

Ruby stared round the soggy garden. The rain had almost stopped, and she

had to squint as the sun peeked through the clouds. A flash of movement darted out from behind a tree.

"Muddle!" Ruby said happily, running after the little puppy. "I thought we'd lost you. Come on – let's go inside for tea."

But the little puppy had gone. In his place, lying on the damp grass, was an old oil lamp. Ruby picked it up.

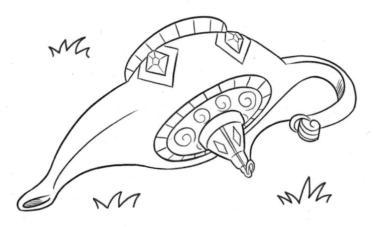

"It's Princess Amber's magic lamp," she said. "We were really there! We'll never forget our adventure now."

"I hope we see Muddle again," said Harry.

"Maybe he'll come back next time it rains," Ruby said, as they walked back up the garden path to Grandad's cottage. As Ruby turned to close the door she gazed out over the garden one last time. The little puppy was nowhere to be seen.

"Goodbye, Muddle," she called out softly. "Come and see us again soon ..."

Can't wait to find out
what Muddle will do next?
Then read on! Here is the first
chapter from Muddle's second
adventure, Toyshop Trouble ...

Muddle
The Magic Puppy

TOYSHOP TROUBLE

"Look at all these toys!" Ruby gasped. She and her cousin Harry were in Grandad's lounge, peering inside an old toy chest. Ruby could see a jumble of model trains and aeroplanes, marbles and motorcars. They were the toys Grandad had played with when he was

a little boy.

"What do you think that is?" Harry asked, pushing his glasses up the bridge of his nose and pointing to a gleaming red-and-green object.

"Let's have a look," Ruby said, leaning so far into the toy chest that only her feet were sticking out. She moved aside a big wooden truck, a tank, and some small metal cars that got tangled in her long braids. Then she grabbed the green-and-red toy and passed it to Harry.

"It's a clockwork train," Harry said, his eyes shining. At the front of the train was the engine, and there were three carriages behind it.

"It's the 2:15 from Paddington,"
Ruby said, "and Teddy is going to
visit Chips!" Teddy was Ruby's toy
duck-billed platypus. He had a long,
furry brown body, four big feet and

a beak like a duck's. Stitched to his bottom was a new pink tail Ruby's mother had sewn on after a tug-of-war accident.

Ruby sat Teddy on one of the carriages and Harry turned the key in the top of the train and set it on the carpet. It chugged across the room in the direction of Chips, Harry's toy robot.

"Go, Teddy!" Ruby said.

Tappety, tappety, tap. The train ran into a desk leg and ground to a halt, but the noise of drumming carried on.

Tappety, tappety, tap.

Ruby leapt up in excitement. "It's raining!" she cried, running to look at

the raindrops pitter-pattering against the windows. Ruby could feel bubbles of excitement fizzing up inside her. The last time it rained, a little puppy called Muddle had arrived, and they had all been swept away on an amazing magical adventure!

The back door blew open, hitting the kitchen worktop with a bang. A bundle of fur zoomed into the room like a rocket, knocked over the clockwork train, Chips and Teddy, and leapt into the toy box. It landed – plumpf – on the toys inside.

"Muddle!" Ruby shouted, clapping her hands with delight.

Ruby and Harry looked inside the

toy box to see a little puppy staring
back at them. His pink tongue was
lolling out and his tail wagged happily.

Harry patted Muddle on the head.
"I'd forgotten what a naughty puppy
he is."

"He's pretending to be a toy!" Ruby

said, laughing. She scooped him up in her arms. "He's definitely as cuddly as Teddy."

"Woof! Woof!" barked Muddle, as if he agreed. Then he wriggled free, dashed across the room, through the kitchen, and into the rainy garden.

Muddle
The Magic Puppy

"Come on!" Ruby shouted with excitement. They rushed after him.

Outside, Muddle bounded down the garden path, splashing in the puddles. His tail was wagging so hard that a blur of raindrops sprayed out. Ruby held out her hands to catch some of the sparkling drops. From behind his glasses, Harry's eyes were shining.

Muddle stopped in front of a particularly large pool of water and raced round and round it. The raindrops were making the surface ripple and shimmer. He crouched down, then jumped into the water with a splash – and disappeared right through the puddle. Just like last time.

Ruby grinned at Harry. "Are
you ready for our next adventure?"
she asked.

"We won't know until we try," Ruby
said. "One, two, three – JUMP!"

And they leapt into the puddle.

***

To be continued ...

Muddle
The Magic Puppy